W9-BRE-223

# the DISAPPEARING MAGICIAN

*the Magic Shop*

# the DISAPPEARING MAGICIAN

the Magic Shop

# MAGICIAN

### Kate Egan
### with Magician Mike Lane

### illustrated by Eric Wight

A ♥

Greenwood Public Library 4.1
310 S. Meridian St.
Greenwood, IN 46143 2

f&F
FEIWEL AND FRIENDS

NEW YORK

Magic Shop #4

A FEIWEL AND FRIENDS BOOK
An Imprint of Macmillan

THE DISAPPEARING MAGICIAN. Text copyright © 2015 by Kate Egan
and Mike Lane. Illustrations copyright © 2015 by Eric Wight. All rights
reserved. Printed in the United States of America by R. R. Donnelley &
Sons Company, Harrisonburg, Virginia. For information, address Feiwel
and Friends, 175 Fifth Avenue, New York, N.Y. 10010.

Feiwel and Friends books may be purchased for business or
promotional use. For information on bulk purchases, please contact
the Macmillan Corporate and Premium Sales Department at (800)
221-7945 x5442 or by e-mail at specialmarkets@macmillan.com.

Library of Congress Cataloging-in-Publication Data Available

ISBN: 978-1-250-02917-1 [hardcover] / 978-1-250-06322-9 [paperback]
978-1-250-08016-5 [ebook]

Book design by Véronique Lefèvre Sweet

Feiwel and Friends logo designed by Filomena Tuosto

First Edition: 2015

1 3 5 7 9 10 8 6 4 2

mackids.com

To my magical friends, the Pols kids.
—K. E.

To my 6-year-old self, who loved magic,
pursued it, and never, ever stopped believing!
—M. L.

# Chapter 1
# READING BUDDIES

**M**ike Weiss had his eyes fixed on the class-room clock. It was 1:58. The minute hand lurched forward, it seemed, about once an hour. When would it be 2:00, then? Some people would say two minutes. Mike knew it would be *forever.*

Mrs. Canfield's fourth graders were gath-ered in a circle as she talked about different kinds of rocks. Some kids were passing rocks around the room: One had layers in it, like stripes, while another one was studded with shells. Yet another one was black and shiny.

"Who can remind me how sedimentary rock is formed?" Mrs. Canfield asked the class.

Who can remind me, Mike wondered, what that is? Or why I need to know?

His eyes wandered back to the clock. 1:59.

Eventually, the rock talk would be over and his class could go downstairs to meet their first-grade book buddies. Reading stories

with pictures to a bunch of little kids . . . *that* was Mike's kind of schoolwork. From now on, they'd get to do it once a week.

"Mike?" said Mrs. Canfield.

He blinked. "Yes?"

"Still with us?"

He sat up straight, like he'd been paying close attention.

Mrs. Canfield prompted him. "Sedimentary rock comes from . . ."

Mike cleared his throat. The whole class was watching.

Next to him, Emily Winston's hand shot up like a rocket. Mike didn't know the answer, but Emily did, and she could hardly wait to blurt it out.

Then there was a *click* from the clock. The minute hand jumped ahead!

Mrs. Canfield stood up and smiled. "We'll get back to this tomorrow," she told the class.

"Two o'clock. Time to go! Our book buddies will be waiting."

Lucky break, Mike thought. Just in time!

There was a rush of activity as the kids stuffed their backpacks with folders and notebooks, lunchboxes and sneakers, so they'd be ready to go home at the end of the day. Then everyone lined up at the door to walk downstairs. It wasn't easy, but Mike managed not to speak above a whisper in the hallway. That was the rule, and he wasn't taking any risks.

Mike tried really hard not to get in trouble at school these days. If he went to the principal's office, she'd call Mike's parents. And if Ms. Scott called his parents, he'd lose an important privilege: biking downtown, all by himself, to The White Rabbit. The world's best magic shop.

The fourth graders filed into Mrs. Kavanaugh's room and stood in a row. The first graders observed them, quiet as mice, from their tiny chairs. Who would he be paired with? Mike wondered. The girl in the unicorn shirt? The boy with the glasses?

The classroom was bright and cheerful, with kids' art all over the wall. On a table in the back, Mike spotted a jumbo bag of pretzels and two bottles of apple juice. Snacks! Mike thought. The afternoon was looking even better. He clutched the book he'd brought to read to his buddy. Sometimes he liked little kids, like his cousins Jake and Lily, better than kids his own age.

"Welcome, fourth graders!" said Mrs. Kavanaugh. "Are we ready to get started?" She passed around a cardboard box, and each of Mike's classmates selected a name from it.

When it was Mike's turn, he stuck his hand in the box and read the name out loud. "Lucas?" he asked, scanning the faces in front of him. A boy with long, shaggy hair raised his hand. "That's me!" he called out. He and Mike walked to the snack table together.

Mike took charge of the apple juice, and unfolded his getting-to-know-you worksheet. This was supposed to make the first grader feel at home with him. "Do you have any pets?" Mike asked. "What are their names?"

Lucas just sat there with his mouth hanging open. His two front teeth were missing.

Can he talk? Mike wondered. It might be hard with missing teeth.

Can he eat pretzels? Mike wasn't sure what to do. Break the snacks into pieces?

"Maybe we should just start reading," he

said. The book he'd brought was called *The Magic Hat*. He was pretty sure a first grader would like it. Mike showed Lucas the cover.

"I knew it!" said Lucas, just about jumping out of his seat. "You're the magician!"

"I do like magic. . . ." Mike admitted.

"I saw you on the playground!" Lucas said. "When I was waiting for the bus!"

He must have seen the Great Escape, Mike realized. With that illusion, he'd tricked Jackson Jacobs, the meanest kid in school!

Lucas was really excited. "I saw you in the lunchroom, too!" he insisted. "You're famous!"

Suddenly, Mike felt two feet taller. Famous? He liked the sound of that. Too bad he didn't see what was coming next.

"Could you do a trick for me?" asked Lucas.

Mike looked around the room. All the names had been chosen and all the kids had broken up into pairs. Mrs. Kavanaugh and

Mrs. Canfield were moving around slowly, making sure the getting-to-know-yous were going well.

I'm supposed to make Lucas feel comfortable, Mike thought. And nobody said I *couldn't* do magic.

He was trying so hard to do everything right! When magic was involved, though, Mike couldn't help himself.

As usual, he had a deck of cards in his pocket. He pulled the cards out and held the four jacks in front of him, like a fan. "See these jacks?" he said to Lucas. "I'm going to put them right here on top of the deck."

"Okay," said Lucas, watching.

Mike put the four jacks on top of the deck and lifted the first one off again. "Now, I'm going to place this jack someplace inside the deck," he said. He stuck it in with the other cards at random and continued, "I'll do that

with the other jacks, too."

Next, he handed the deck to Lucas. "Can you hold these for a second?" When Lucas got hold of them, Mike said, "Now, take the four cards off the top for me, okay?"

Lucas's jaw dropped as he peeled off four jacks in a row.

"Voila," said Mike, scooping the cards out of his hands and wishing, like always, that he had a good magic word. "The four jacks jumped to the top!"

"That's *sick*," Lucas said in awe.

Mike looked over at Mrs. Canfield. She was talking to Oscar and heading in his direction. Mike stuck the cards back in his pocket.

"I think we should start the book now, okay?" he said to Lucas.

The story was about a wizard, not a magician. He had a hat that could make him invisible and allow him to fly. It could make

# JUMPING JACKS

**1.**

$\mathcal{S}$ TART BY REMOVING THE FOUR JACKS FROM A DECK OF CARDS AND HOLDING THEM OUT, LIKE A FAN, TO SHOW YOUR AUDIENCE.

WHAT YOUR AUDIENCE DOESN'T KNOW IS THAT YOU HAVE HIDDEN FOUR RANDOM CARDS BEHIND THE FAN. HOLD THESE CARDS AT THE BACK OF THE FAN WITH YOUR THUMB, WHILE USING THE REST OF YOUR FINGERS TO HOLD THE VISIBLE CARDS AT THE FRONT.

**2.**

THEN, WITH BOTH HANDS, BRING THE JACKS TOGETHER, KEEPING THE RANDOM CARDS HIDDEN BEHIND THEM.

**3.**

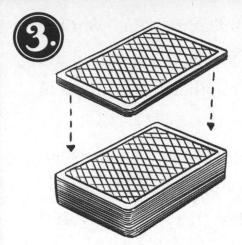

NEXT YOU'LL PUT THE EIGHT CARDS—WHICH THE AUDIENCE THINKS ARE JUST FOUR—FACE-DOWN ON TOP OF THE DECK.

**4.**

REMOVE THE TOP CARD—WHICH YOU KNOW TO BE RANDOM—AND TELL YOUR AUDIENCE "I WILL PLACE THIS JACK SOMEWHERE IN THE DECK." DO EXACTLY THE SAME THING WITH THE NEXT THREE CARDS. BE CAREFUL NOT TO SHOW THE AUDIENCE THE FACES OF THE CARDS!

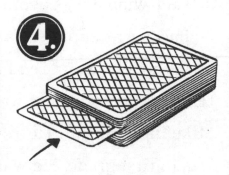

**5.**

WAVE YOUR HAND DRAMATICALLY OVER THE WHOLE DECK. THEN TURN OVER THE TOP FOUR CARDS TO SHOW THAT THE JACKS HAVE "JUMPED" TO THE TOP OF THE DECK! LET THE AUDIENCE LOOK THROUGH THE DECK TO BE SURE THAT YOU HAD ONLY FOUR JACKS TO START WITH.

stuff appear and disappear, too. But even the wizard didn't know it could shoot red-hot lightning bolts—until another wizard tried to steal it!

Lucas's mouth dropped open again when the wizards met. He gripped the desk till the magic hat saved the day. "Let's read it again!" he said when it was over.

Lucas was supposed to read a book of his own, though. "Sun," read Lucas slowly. "Rain." His book had only one word on each page, but Mike didn't mind. He remembered when he was in first grade. He wasn't good at reading, either.

When their time was up, Lucas didn't want to say good-bye. "See you next week, buddy," Mike said, with a light punch to his shoulder. Lucas beamed, and for a minute Mike felt like he really *was* famous.

Mrs. Canfield's class trooped back upstairs

just as the end-of-the-day announcements began. Mike was only half-listening, as usual. If there was anything important, his parents would tell him.

"Now for some news that will brighten the dark winter days!" Mrs. Warren, the school secretary, said cheerfully.

Why were grown-ups always talking about making the winter better? Mike wondered. He and his friends loved the winter! But grown-ups didn't play outside in the snow.

Mrs. Warren went on. "On Monday, we will start putting together our first-ever talent show!"

A talent show? The announcement was like an electric shock.

Now Mike was listening hard.

Mrs. Warren continued, "Bring your act, ready to perform, to the gym after school on Monday afternoon. This is not an audition,

but an open call for acts. We will spend the week rehearsing, with the big show Friday night!" Then she moved onto another announcement about the Lost and Found.

Mike wasn't always into school activities. And okay, it wasn't like anyone was begging him to join the school clubs. But he actually had a talent, the kind he could show onstage! Chess Club kids couldn't say that, could they?

Some people, like Lucas, had seen Mike's magic already. But he could do so much more! What if he didn't have to steal time during class? What if he had a stage all to himself? Then he'd *really* be famous! Just like his distant relative, Harry Houdini.

Suddenly, the coming weekend was full of purpose. Mike would pick out his best magic, practice with Nora, plan his show.

It was time to get his act together!

## Chapter 2
## A SURPRISE

**A**t their usual meet-up spot on the playground, Mike waited for Nora. Where was she, anyway? Chatting with her teacher like they were BFFs? Asking for extra homework? Sometimes, Nora did things that Mike would never understand.

It was starting to snow, so he zipped up his jacket and put on his hat. Then he stuck out his tongue to catch some snowflakes. Each one was like a tiny drink of water.

Some kids were lining up for the bus, but others—like Mike—were lingering on the playground before walking home.

There was a patch of ice right in the middle of the basketball court, with kids sliding around on it in their boots. There was also a giant snowbank, built up by plows after each storm. Right now, it was as high as the second floor of the school! Other kids were busy with a snowball war up there. But none of them was Nora.

Mike had to tell her about the talent show! If he didn't say it out loud, he was going to burst! Was she playing at the edge of the woods? Someone had built a fort back there, he knew.

He was walking toward it when a figure in head-to-toe snow gear, a cloud of steam coming out of its mouth, yelled "Mike! Come check out the slide!"

Mike didn't even know who it was—in winter coats and snowpants, you could barely tell who was a boy and who was a girl. It wasn't Nora, he was sure. But what was he supposed to do while he was waiting for her? Curiously, he followed the mystery kid.

Turned out it was Mike's new friend Adam. His hat flew off as he whipped down the slide three times faster than usual, along a thick layer of ice. He crash-landed at the bottom, laughed, and said to Mike, "You've gotta try it!"

Might as well, Mike thought.

It was faster than a zipline! Faster than a roller coaster! Soon, a line of boys was gathered there, taking turns and perfecting the ride. "It's better like this!" said Mike's friend Charlie, tucking his legs up as he slid. "Or this!" yelled someone else, going down

headfirst. Even Mike could tell that it wasn't completely safe. He really wanted to try it . . . but what if he got hurt before the talent show?

Mike was at the top rung of the steps, about to lie down on the slide, when he noticed a purple coat across the playground. It was Nora, with a bunch of girls, making a snowman.

Finally!

Mike zipped down the slide with his arms out. "Later," he said to the boys.

Nora was sticking rocks along the front of the snowman, like buttons, while Coco—from Nora's class—unwound her own scarf to wrap around its neck.

"Now all he needs is a nose!" Nora said. She spotted Mike and waved.

"Looks great," Mike said. He couldn't wait to get out of here! "Ready to go?"

She said, "Almost. I just need to find a carrot."

"A carrot?" Mike repeated. Was she serious?

"From someone's leftover lunch," Nora explained. "Or the cafeteria, maybe. For the nose."

On some other day, Mike might have liked that kind of treasure hunt. But not today! And it was impossible, right? Why would you leave carrots in your lunchbox, if you'd been unlucky enough to get them? They'd be in the trash by now.

"I need to tell you something!" he whispered urgently.

Nora looked at him. "Can't you tell me right here?"

"No!" Mike said. He looked around to make sure no one was watching. "It's a magic thing, okay?" They had planning to do, and practicing. In secret! It was much more important than a snowman's nose!

"I'm not ready yet," Nora said firmly. "I could meet you at home."

What would Mike say to his mom and dad? He couldn't leave Nora behind. They were supposed to stick together if they didn't have after-school activities.

"No, I'll stay," he said, frowning. He jammed his fingers into his pockets and waited while Nora and Coco—plus Ellie and Ana—put the finishing touches on their snowman. Instead of a carrot, they ended up using an orange marker.

Okay, he was an awesome snowman, Mike had to admit. But did it really have to take so long? He'd probably be melted by Monday.

When they finally left the playground, Mike and Nora were cold and wet. Pretty soon, it would be dark.

"What's the rush? What's so important?" Nora said as they hurried across the street.

"Did you hear about the talent show?" Mike blurted out. "We can do a magic act! And I've already been thinking about the tricks. We can do the Balloon Pop and the Coin Drop. Plus some others, I guess. The first practice is after school on Monday." He was talking so fast, he was already out of breath.

All Mike could hear was the sound of Nora's boots, crunching in the snow.

She was much too quiet.

Sometimes Nora's family went away on the weekends, skiing or to museums in Boston. "Will you be here?" he asked nervously.

Nora's boots kept crunching. "I think so," she said. She was a little ahead of him, not meeting his gaze. "It's just that . . . what if I don't want to be in the talent show, Mike?"

Was she speaking a foreign language? "Why wouldn't you want to be in the talent show?" he asked.

But he already knew the answer. It was all

his fault! He'd rushed her off the playground, and now she was mad.

"I'm really sorry!" Mike said, trying to keep up with her. "I was so excited. I couldn't wait to tell you!"

"No, it's not that," said Nora. She was staring at the sidewalk. "I just don't like the whole idea. It's pretty different from doing magic on the playground, you know? At night, in the gym, with people's parents there . . . I have stage fright just thinking about it."

Mike's jaw dropped, like Lucas's.

Did she really just say that?

"There's nothing to be afraid of," he said in a rush. "It's our big chance! We'll be the center of attention in a *good* way. We'll amaze the whole school!"

He thought about standing on the stage in the gym. He'd been there before, for school concerts. The music teacher was always mouthing the same words, pointing to her eyes: "Look at me, Mike. Focus!"

In the talent show, though, he could do things his own way. Mike wasn't usually overflowing with confidence, but he had confidence in this. He knew he could do it. It could be the best act in the whole show, he thought. He really needed Nora!

"You have to be in the talent show," he said desperately. "We're partners!"

Nora finally turned to look at him. "Partners decide *together*," she said. "And I don't want to do it."

For the rest of their walk, there was an icy silence. Then Nora walked up the stairs to his house and opened the door like nothing was wrong. Talk about a great performance.

Mike's dad smiled at her, as usual. His parents loved Nora. Mr. Weiss made hot chocolate

and asked them questions about their day. "I met my new book buddy," Nora said politely. She didn't look at Mike, or mention the talent show. She asked what Mike's dad was cooking for dinner. "Smells delicious," she said, and suddenly Mike's dad was sharing his secret recipe for hamburgers.

Nora doesn't care about impressing kids at school, Mike thought. She impresses people every day. Even her snowman was perfect! Everything she does is magic.

It was different for him, though. He had only one talent—and only one chance to show it off for a crowd.

Couldn't Nora see that? Maybe she wasn't as smart as he thought.

She's not going to stop me, Mike thought suddenly. She *can't* stop me!

He'd thought that Nora was the perfect partner. Trustworthy, smart, and fun.

But she's not the only partner out there, right? Mike thought.

If I can't have Nora, I'll just have to find someone else.

## Chapter 3
# PLAYDATE

**E**very Saturday morning, Mike was secretly glad his parents had made him quit soccer. No more early practice. No more games in the rain. Mike had spent the whole soccer season settling into a great Saturday pattern. He hung around in his pajamas while his parents went to the gym, or got some work done on their computers. Another bowl of cereal,

another half hour of cartoons. Then he practiced magic for the rest of the day.

But today, Mike was flipping through the
school directory before his parents were even
awake. When his mom came downstairs to
start the coffee, he was waiting at the kitchen
table. "Can I have a friend over?" he asked.

Mrs. Weiss rubbed her eyes. "Fine by me,"
she said. "Isn't it a little early?"

Mike waited until exactly nine o'clock.
Then he picked up the phone and punched in
Adam's number.

Turned out he was free all day.

Which would give Mike all day to ask if
he'd be in the talent show.

It was always weird to have a friend over
for the first time, Mike thought. There wasn't
a thing that the two of you always did together,
like video games or shooting baskets. A little

later, a little awkwardly, Mike showed Adam around his house.

Suddenly, Mike saw everything through his friend's eyes. His room was a disaster! There were piles of clothes on the floor. Maybe he should have thrown away some of his papers from school.

Adam didn't seem to care, though. He admired the Red Sox pennant that Mike's dad had gotten him at Fenway Park. He took Mike's Lego space station off the dresser and said "Awesome!" And when Mike opened his closet, Adam's eyes bugged out. "Whoa!" he said. "It's like the magic shop in there!"

Mike's closet was super-organized. His mom had picked up some plastic bins for him, and his dad had installed some shelves, all to keep his magic stuff straight. No one could make magic out of a mess! Most of Mike's magic called for ordinary stuff like cups and

bottles, or cards or pens, and all those things had their own place. Mike's closet was even neater than Nora's!

"No one at school would believe it, right?" said Mike.

Adam laughed. "No way."

"So, can I show you something?" Mike asked him.

"Something magic?" said Adam. He sounded hopeful, Mike thought. Which made *him* hopeful that Adam would say yes . . . when he finally got around to asking him.

Why was he putting it off?

Well, what if Adam said no?

Mike went into his closet and opened a bag of balloons. He took out a red one, stretched it out, and blew it up. He held it so Adam could see. "A regular old balloon," he told his friend. "Like you might have at your birthday party."

Adam looked it over. "Okay," he said.

Then Mike took a long pin out of the cup of pencils on his desk. "Watch this," he told Adam. Mike waved the pin through the air dramatically. Then he pushed it through the balloon, but it didn't pop.

"That's strange," Mike said. He tried again. "I don't know what's going on."

He looked at Adam. "Want to try it yourself?"

Adam was eager. "Sure!" he said. He took the pin from Mike and plunged it into the balloon. It popped right away, and blasted into several pieces that flew around the room.

"Everything okay?" called Mike's mom from downstairs.

"Everything's fine," Mike yelled back.

Adam looked at the pin, like he was trying to figure it out. "So what's magic about this pin?" he said. "Why didn't it pop the balloon when you used it?"

Mike took a deep breath. Real magicians never explained their illusions.

But Adam already knew how Mike pulled off the Great Escape, right? Together, he and Nora had concealed Mike from Jackson!

And Mike was going to have to share a few more tricks of the trade if he wanted Adam's help in the show.

Mike dropped his voice, even though no one else was listening. "The trick isn't in the pin at all. It's in the balloon."

Mike took a blue balloon from the bag and blew it up like before. "Now watch this," he said. He slipped a tiny piece of tape onto the balloon, then covered it quickly with his hand. "The audience doesn't know it's there," Mike said. "But this is where you put the pin."

# BALLOON POP

**1.** *B*EFORE YOU PERFORM, YOU'LL WANT TO BLOW UP A BALLOON, TIE IT AT THE BOTTOM, AND STICK A SMALL PIECE OF CLEAR TAPE ON IT. WHEN YOU SHOW THE BALLOON TO YOUR AUDIENCE, BE SURE NOT TO SHOW THEM THE PART WITH THE TAPE.

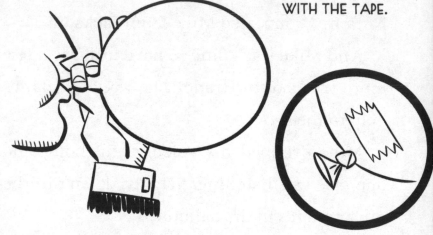

**2.** WITH THE BALLOON IN ONE HAND, PICK UP A LONG PIN WITH THE OTHER. WAVE THE PIN SLOWLY IN THE AIR, BACK AND FORTH, TO MAKE YOUR AUDIENCE CURIOUS ABOUT WHAT WILL HAPPEN NEXT.

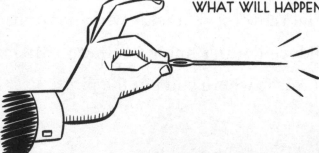

**3.**

THEN, TAKE THE PIN AND PIERCE
THE BALLOON THROUGH THE
TAPE. IT WON'T POP!

**4.**

POP!

BEFORE YOU LEAVE THE
STAGE, THROW THE BALLOON
IN THE AIR AND POP IT WITH THE
PIN. THAT WAY, NO ONE WILL KNOW
YOUR SECRET!

Adam was staring at the tape. "Wait! How did you get that on there, a minute ago, without me noticing?"

Mike grinned. "A little conversation," he said. "Remember I said it was like a balloon from a birthday party? That was to distract you for a second."

Adam shook his head. "I can't believe I didn't see it!"

Mike returned to the trick. "If you put the pin in through the tape, it's guaranteed the balloon won't pop. But when anyone else tries it, they put the pin in someplace else, and the balloon pops right away."

"Wicked cool," Adam said.

Now or never, Mike thought. He took a deep breath and changed the subject. "So, did you hear about the school talent show?" he asked.

"Yeah," said Adam, reaching for another balloon. "I wish I had a talent."

"You don't have any talents at all?" Mike said. It was too good to be true!

"I like playing the recorder in music class," Adam said. "But everyone in the whole fourth grade can do that. And I'm a good swimmer but, you know, I can't exactly swim in the gym."

"I'm going to do a magic act," Mike said. "It's going to be awesome. The thing is . . . I need someone to help me out." At first, he didn't look at Adam. But when Mike stole a glance at his friend, his expression was easy to read. Adam looked like he'd just won the lottery!

"Really?" Adam said. "Like a magician's assistant?"

"Sort of," Mike explained. "But not the kind of assistant that gets sawed in half or anything like that. You'd help me set things up, get things off the stage. . . ." That sounded too boring! "You'd learn a lot of magic, too," Mike promised.

"Sure!" Adam said. "I'll do it! Definitely!"

Great! thought Mike. But there was one more thing.

Magicians swore an oath not to tell their secrets. "You know, you can't tell anyone what you see or hear," he said uncomfortably. Mike didn't want to scare Adam off, but this was important.

Adam didn't hesitate. "I know," he said. "You can trust me. Remember when we did that trick on the playground with Nora?" Then he remembered something else. "Hey, what about Nora? Is she in the act, too?"

"She's . . . super-busy," Mike told him. He didn't want Adam to get stage fright, too!

He walked to his closet and took out one of the bins. "So, you want to get started?"

## Chapter 4
# PARTNERS

**M**ike knew two great tricks that worked the same way. For both of them, he'd use a black thread—that the audience couldn't see—to make something move mysteriously. For one trick, it was a ring borrowed from a member of the audience. For the other, it was a pen in a bottle.

"I've practiced them over and over, but I've never performed them for people," Mike told Adam. "They're not the sort of tricks you can do up close, like in a classroom. You need to be a little further away from the audience, like on a stage, so no one sees how they work. I've never been on a real stage before!"

Just saying that gave him goose bumps.

"I can get a ring from someone in the audience," Adam said helpfully.

"Good!" said Mike. "While you do that, I'll take a pen out of my pocket."

The pen would be all prepared ahead of time, he explained, with a thread wrapped around the tip, stuck in place with tape, and covered by the pen cap. The other end of the thread would be around a button on his shirt.

Mike added, "When you give me the ring, I'll drop it onto the pen. Then I'll move the pen away from my body, and the ring will move upward. It will defy gravity! That's what the audience will think, anyway. Really, it will be traveling on the thread."

He showed Adam what he was talking about. Then he demonstrated a similar illusion: making a pen "rise" through an empty plastic bottle.

While one part of him was doing the trick for Adam, another part of him was watching something outside through his bedroom window. There was a car pulling into Nora's driveway. There was Nora, skipping out of her house, getting in the car, and going who-knew-where, with who-knew-who. Could Mike really do a show without her?

His glance fell on his dresser next. *The Book of Secrets* was buried in there, along with a lot of mismatched socks. It would be easier if Adam could just read the directions, Mike thought. Then he wouldn't have to describe each step of every magic trick. But Mike wasn't ready to share his book—yet—with anyone but Nora.

"So, do you have a black shirt?" Mike asked Adam.

"I'm not sure," he said. "I don't think so."

"That could be a problem," said Mike. He had a real magician's shirt, himself. It was all black, with buttons down the front, and a pocket on the chest. His grandma had given him the shirt at Christmas, and he hadn't even worn it yet!

He took it out of his closet. "The pen goes in the pocket, see?" he said. "And the color hides the black thread."

Mike thought about how he and Adam would look onstage. Did they want to look like a couple of fourth graders? Or did they want to look like real magicians? When they ran through their act on Monday, they needed to be convincing.

"Know what?" Mike said. "I think you need one of these, too."

"Okay, sure," said Adam agreeably. "Where do I get one, though?"

Mike acted like it was no big deal to go to his favorite place. "I guess we'll have to go to The White Rabbit!" He'd lend Adam some money, and Adam could pay him back.

It was too icy to ride bikes, but Mike's mom agreed to drop them off while she picked up some groceries. Even when it was cold outside, Mike had a warm feeling when he opened the store's front door.

Carlos was up front, using magic to link and unlink a pair of metal rings. "Coming back to your home away from home?" he teased Mike. Eliot and Jasmine, some other teenagers who worked for Mr. Zerlin, were carrying a red velvet couch for a customer. "Hey, Mike!" they both called out.

Now Adam knew that Mike belonged here.

Mike led his friend to the back of the store, to the room that said "Secrets Inside." Adam went "Whoa!" when he saw the shelves piled high with new stuff. There was a six-foot pole that could appear out of nowhere, and a set of foam mice that a magician could multiply endlessly. There was even a magic wand that would break apart the minute a magician handed it to someone else!

"I think the shirts are over here," Mike said, peering into a corner. He took one off a rack and brought it over to Adam. His friend was holding a Magic 8 Ball. "Hey, let's ask it a question!" Adam said. "How about . . . will we rock the talent show?"

He shook it and turned it over to see the message it revealed: "Without a doubt!"

WITHOUT A DOUBT

"I'm totally getting this thing," Adam said. "You have one, too, right?"

Mike nodded. He loved his Magic 8 Ball, but he could have made that prediction himself!

He held the shirt up to Adam, the way his mom did when she was trying to figure out if something would fit him. "This looks about right," he said. "Maybe you should try it on?" Okay, he actually had no clue if there was a changing room here. "Um, follow me."

Mike opened a door that turned out to be a closet. He stepped behind a curtain that had a stack of boxes behind it. "I think the best place is downstairs," Mike said like he knew.

He'd only been in the basement once before, and that was with Carlos. A part of him wondered if it was off-limits. He led the way to the steps. What would he say to Adam if they got in trouble?

When they arrived in the basement, Adam was as surprised as Mike had been the first time he saw it. It was set up like a small theater, with comfortable chairs and a real curtain. "Imagine being on *this* stage," Adam said in a low voice.

Mike had already imagined it a million times.

There wasn't a changing room down here, either. But as Mike's eyes grew used to the dim light, he could see a figure on the stage, Mr. Zerlin. He was wearing a black shirt with a magic wand embroidered on the front. His wild hair was tame today, like he'd brushed it for once.

Mr. Zerlin was just standing there, shuffling a deck of cards. Was he thinking? Or meditating? Or planning something for his new act? You never knew with Mr. Zerlin.

"Sorry," said Mike. "Didn't mean to bother you."

The cards fell into a tidy pile in Mr. Zerlin's hands. "Mike!" he said, all friendly. He didn't seem to mind that they were there.

Mike introduced Adam, and explained, "We're just here to get him a shirt. We're doing a magic act for the talent show at school!"

Mr. Zerlin took off his glasses and looked at Mike. "A talent show?" he said with interest. "That's good news. You'll show the whole school what you've learned!" He totally got it!

Mike rushed to tell him more. "I'm still trying to decide what we'll do," he said. "The Balloon Pop, definitely. And the Rising Ring and the Floating Pen. Something with my magic hat, I'm thinking. And for the grand finale . . . Well, I don't know yet. Something that will knock their socks off."

Mr. Zerlin had traveled all over the world with his act—and his partner, Cam—before he settled in to run the store. If only he could help! Mike thought suddenly. What if he had a great idea for the grand finale?

Mr. Zerlin focused all his attention on the boys, his blue eyes bright. He raised his eyebrows like he was about to say something important. "Can I give you a tip?" he asked.

Mike held his breath. "Sure," he said.

Adam broke in nervously, "The show is next Friday," he said. "We have a lot of practicing to do."

Mr. Zerlin's laugh was soft and low, like a purr. Mike had never heard him laugh before. "That's just what I was going to say!" he told Adam. "Practice is the key to success. Sounds like the two of you will make a good team."

Mike's grandma always said, "Practice makes perfect." Everyone knew that! He'd kind of hoped for a better tip from Mr. Zerlin.

"You need to be able to do your act automatically," the magician continued. "Trust me, there is nothing worse than losing your way onstage." Not that he would even know, Mike thought. Mr. Zerlin never messed up! His magic was flawless.

Mike was already thinking about other places he could find ideas. Not from Nora, not this time. But definitely in *The Book of Secrets*. Or maybe online. He'd found some good ideas there before—

Then Mr. Zerlin drew closer to them, like he didn't want to be overheard. "As for the grand finale," he said. "May I teach you how to do the Disappearing Magician?"

## Chapter 5
# FIRST REHEARSAL

**M**onday morning was pretty awkward. Nora came by as usual, to pick up Mike on her way to school. She smelled like shampoo and toothpaste, ready for a fresh start to the new week. Mike, on the other hand, was putting off a shower for one more day. He hoisted his backpack on and took one last bite of toast.

"Oh, hang on," he said. "I forgot something." He dumped the backpack and ran back to his

room to get the magic hat
his grandma had
given him. Long
ago, it belonged to
Houdini himself!
Mike couldn't
wear it to school—
what if Jackson

Jacobs tried to grab it? But he had to have it for the talent show run-through. It was his most important prop!

Mike tried to make polite conversation on the way to school. "How was your weekend?" he asked Nora.

"Fine," she replied. Obviously, she didn't want to talk.

If anyone is mad, it should be me! Mike thought.

Mike didn't tell Nora about his plans for the talent show. He didn't tell her about Adam, either. She'd find out soon enough, right? He broke away from her as soon as they arrived at school.

♥ ♥ ♥

While Mrs. Canfield went on and on about rocks, Mike's thoughts drifted to his magic act. Had he and Adam put the tricks in the right order? Should they do the Disappearing Magician today, or save it for the real performance? Mike liked the idea of keeping some secrets till Friday night. But how would they practice the trick, then? It was pretty complicated.

"Mike?" said Mrs. Canfield. "Could you tell us where igneous rock comes from?"

"Volcanoes," he answered automatically.

"Nice!" said Mrs. Canfield with a smile. "That's exactly right."

At the end of the day, Mrs. Canfield still remembered his small success. "Good work today, Mike," she said as everyone was leaving. "Must have been hard to stay focused with the talent show coming up. Are you doing a magic act? I can't wait to see what you come up with!"

"You're going to love it!" Mike promised. Then he rushed to the gym so fast that he almost fell down the stairs.

Adam was there, sitting on the shiny floor with a bunch of other nervous kids. There was a kindergarten boy trying to juggle, and a group of fifth-grade girls lip-synching to a song on someone's phone. There was even a pair of mimes!

What was with the cheerleaders in the corner? Mike wondered. Was that their talent, or was there going to be some kind of game? And who was in those crazy chicken costumes?

They were all wearing masks and feather boas.

Everyone got quiet when Mrs. Warren walked to the front of the gym. The school secretary ran the school office—but she ran almost everything else, too. Mike knew her well. Anyone going to see the principal had to wait at her desk.

"Eyes up here," Mrs. Warren said, waving her arms so no one could miss her. "Are we ready to begin?" Her microphone came on with a shriek.

To start with, she laid out some ground rules. "We've never had a talent show at this school before," she explained. "But we want to make it an annual event."

"Woo-hoo!" yelled one of the cheerleaders.

"I'll need your cooperation with a few things, though," Mrs. Warren continued.

The kids in each act had to attend the

rehearsals all week. They'd be held after school every day, right here on the stage in the gym. Tonight, Mrs. Warren would put the acts in some kind of order, and each day, they would run through the whole set.

"My team will work on sound and lighting," Mrs. Warren explained. "So, you won't have to worry about those details. But you will be responsible for your own costumes and make-up. And for being here on time." She looked around to make sure everyone was listening.

"Now, for the most important thing," said Mrs. Warren. "The purpose of this show is to spread school spirit, make us proud of all the talent we have in our student body. There are no prizes and no judges, because this is not a competition. And this is not an audition, either. Anyone can take part if they are brave enough to go onstage."

She waited for her message to sink in. "We all support one another and appreciate the hard work of other students. Booing and bullying will not be tolerated. Is that clear?"

Mike nodded along with everyone else. If it were a competition, he'd have wanted first place. If there wasn't a prize, though, what did he want? To stand out from everyone else, he thought. To amaze the audience. To blow their minds!

Adam passed him a clipboard. "Here, we have to write our names down," he explained.

In big writing, Mike scrawled "Mike Weiss, Man of Magic" at the bottom of the list. Adam added "With his absolutely astonishing assistant, Adam Abbott." Then he returned the clipboard to Mrs. Warren.

"Thank you," she said. "So, how about we take it from the top?"

Mrs. Warren looked at the first name on the list. "Lucas, come on up and show us your talent!" It was Mike's book buddy! As he dragged a tall, wooden stool onto the stage, Mike put two fingers in his mouth and whistled. "Go, Lucas!" he yelled. That was supportive, right?

Then Lucas sat on the stool and started cracking jokes.

"Why did the boy steal a chair from the classroom?" he asked. He waited a minute, then answered his own question, laughing. "Because the teacher told him to take a seat!" With his hands, Lucas clapped three beats on the side of the stool. *Ba-dum-dum.*

"What do ghosts serve for dessert?" Again, he paused. "Ice scream and booberries!" *Ba-dum-dum.*

Altogether, Lucas told about ten jokes, and everyone clapped as he bounded down the stairs. If Mike had a pom-pom, he would have cheered with the cheerleaders. No way he would have gone onstage when he was in first grade! Lucas was totally awesome.

The next act was Mike's classmate, Will, with his guitar. He played a Beatles tune and sang at the same time. Impressive, Mike thought.

Then the lip-synchers, who acted like they were teenagers already. Then a second-grade girl did cartwheels across the stage.

When the gymnast was finished, Mrs. Warren looked at her clipboard. "Mike Weiss, Man of Magic?" she said. "You're up!" Mike adjusted his black shirt and put on his hat. He grabbed his box of props, and took the stage.

Mike began by saying, "Magic is everywhere, even in places you'd never expect it. Like this balloon, for instance." He stretched it out, blew it up, and held it so the audience could see. "It's like what you'd find at a birthday party, right?"

It was the same patter he'd used when he did the trick for Adam. The audience was so busy smiling and nodding that they didn't notice when he slipped the tape on the back. They were totally paying attention when Adam took out the giant pin, though! All the kids were tense, waiting for a giant *pop*.

Mike put the pin in through the tape, slowly. Suspensefully. And nothing happened! He heard someone gasp in surprise.

He had them.

He had this!

Just as he'd promised, Adam went out into the crowd to get a ring from someone. Okay, Mike wouldn't have picked Mrs. Warren's wedding ring, but all the kids loved it.

"Don't make it disappear!" Lucas called out.

"You'll be in Ms. Scott's office all year if you do!" someone else added.

Were they teasing Mike? Did they know he went to the principal more than most kids?

He didn't know, but he shook it off. Today, he wasn't a troublemaker. Today, he was a Man of Magic!

Once Adam delivered the ring, Mike took a pen from his pocket and dropped the ring over the top. "Now, watch this ring carefully," Mike told the kids. "I will move it with my eyes!" He gave the ring a death stare, and moved the pen away from his body. As he did that, the ring traveled upward on the invisible thread.

Mike really wished he had a good magic word to say right now. Abracadabra was just too . . . predictable. One of these days, he'd come up with something better. Did it even matter, though? People were pretty shocked when they saw the ring move.

Adam knew just what to do next. He set up an empty plastic bottle on a table, and Mike dropped his pen into it. Then he ordered the pen to rise into thin air, and it heeded his magical call. Mike caught it near his chin and walked to the edge of the stage. The other kids were already applauding.

Nora didn't want to be in this show? Well, Mike was just fine without her.

"That's just a taste of what we'll do on Friday night," Mike explained to everyone in the gym. "The best is yet to come!" he declared boldly.

"But you'll be rehearsing your full act with us this week?" Mrs. Warren asked.

Mike didn't want people to figure out the tricks before the real performance.

"I was hoping we could keep some of our secrets . . . secret," he said smoothly.

# The FLOATING PEN

**1.**  BEFORE YOU PERFORM, YOU'LL NEED TO PREPARE A PEN. IT SHOULD BE A BLACK ONE, WITH A CAP THAT GOES OVER THE TOP. TAKE THE CAP OFF, THEN WRAP A LENGTH OF BLACK THREAD AROUND THE POINT MANY TIMES, SECURING IT WITH A PIECE OF CLEAR TAPE. PUT THE CAP BACK ON WHEN YOU'RE DONE.

**2.** NEXT, WRAP THE OTHER END OF THE THREAD AROUND A BUTTON ON YOUR SHIRT. (A BLACK SHIRT WITH A POCKET WILL WORK BEST.) PLACE THE PEN IN THE POCKET.

**3.** YOU WILL ALSO NEED A CLEAR PLASTIC BOTTLE.

WHEN YOU ARE READY TO PERFORM, TAKE THE PEN FROM YOUR POCKET AND HOLD IT OUT IN FRONT OF YOU, WITH THE CAP FACING UP.

HOLDING THE BOTTLE CLOSE TO YOUR BODY, DROP THE PEN INSIDE. AT THIS POINT, THE THREAD WILL BE LOOSE AND SLACK. AS YOU MOVE THE BOTTLE AWAY FROM YOUR BODY, THOUGH, THE THREAD WILL TIGHTEN AND THE PEN WILL RISE INSIDE THE BOTTLE! MAKE A SHOW OF "CONCENTRATING" ON THE PEN, LIKE YOU ARE WILLING IT TO RISE. WHEN THE PEN RISES OUT OF THE TOP, PUT IT RIGHT BACK IN YOUR POCKET. YOUR SECRET WILL BE SAFE FOR YOUR NEXT PERFORMANCE.

# RISING RING
## *Variation*

**1.** To PERFORM THIS TRICK, SOMEONE IN YOUR AUDIENCE WILL NEED TO LEND YOU A RING.

**2.**  TAKE THE PEN FROM YOUR POCKET, AND HOLD IT CLOSE TO YOU WITH THE CAP FACING UP. DROP THE RING OVER THE PEN, ALLOWING IT TO REST ON YOUR FINGERS.

**3.** THEN, SLOWLY MOVE THE PEN AWAY FROM YOUR BODY (AND TOWARD THE AUDIENCE). WAVE YOUR OTHER HAND OVER THE PEN AND SAY SOME MAGIC WORDS! AS THE PEN KEEPS MOVING, THE THREAD WILL GROW TIGHTER. AND AS IT GROWS TIGHTER, THE RING WILL RISE TO THE TOP OF THE PEN!

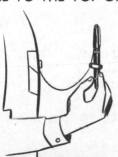

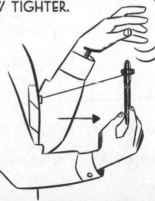

Mrs. Warren nodded and wrote something on her clipboard. "That will be fine, Mike," she said.

As soon as he left the stage, Mike wanted to go back!

"We rocked it," Adam whispered. "Just like the Magic 8 Ball said."

The funky chickens were up next, leading all the kids in their version of the chicken dance. Mike didn't love dancing, but right now, he would dance with anyone who asked! On Friday night, he was going to be a real magician on a real stage!

Only the mimes' act was left, and Mike's backpack was in his classroom. His mom was picking him up soon. Better to get it now, before she got here—she never liked to wait.

Very quietly, Mike opened the gym door and slipped out. He was trying so hard not to disturb the mimes that he didn't notice a chicken on the floor in the hallway ... until he tripped over its legs.

He also noticed that, without its mask on, the chicken looked familiar. Its face was buried in its feathers, but Mike would know that ponytail anywhere.

She'd let him down, and he was disappointed. But what was he supposed to do? He couldn't just walk right by her.

"Nora?" Mike asked. "Are you okay?"

## Chapter 6
# HELPING NORA

**H**er eyes were all red. "What do you think?" she asked.

"Um, I guess not," Mike said. What was she doing here? "*You* were one of the funky chickens?"

"I was," she said. "But I am never, ever doing that again! I'm dropping out of the show, and now Ellie and Ana are mad."

Mike was so confused. "Wait a minute," he said. "I thought you didn't want to *be* in the show!"

Nora blew her nose. "I didn't," she replied. "I don't! But Ellie and Ana asked me, and I thought it might be easier if nobody knew who I was. I think it was even worse! It's scary enough to get up onstage in front of everyone. It's more scary to do it in a stupid costume."

Mike agreed. "Yeah," he said. "It is a pretty stupid costume."

Would he ever learn to think before he opened his big mouth?

But Nora thought it was funny. Actually, she laughed until her eyes teared up again. "Did you see the sequins on the mask?" she giggled. "And the feathers are already coming off this boa. . . . I'm shedding!"

Any minute now, Mike's mom would be here. "Do you want a ride home?" he asked Nora. Maybe things were back to normal.

She said, "My dad is on his way."

"My mom can call him," Mike told her. "Come on!" After his performance, he still felt like flying. He'd do the chicken dance all the way to the parking lot if it would cheer Nora up. His happiness was contagious!

Of course Mike's mom was thrilled to drive Nora home. Before he knew it, they were talking about some new book and he was left out of the conversation. Why couldn't they ever talk about something he'd actually read? *Guinness Book of World Records*, maybe?

So, Mike ran through the act in his mind again. He and Adam still had a lot to work on. But if it went well today, it would be even better on Friday night! He could practically hear the applause already.

Then he thought about Nora's situation. Should she call her friends to talk it over? he wondered.

And then he thought about his act and Nora's situation at the same time.

Until last week, Nora had been his partner in magic.

And she was afraid to be onstage?

Why hadn't she told him that before?

Nora could never be his assistant if she was a scaredy-cat!

Mike and Adam would make the perfect team for the talent show. But what would happen after the show? Mike couldn't leave Nora out of his act forever. She knew all his secrets!

An idea came to Mike as quickly as state capitals came to Nora.

She had helped him tons of times before . . . now *he* had to help *her*. He had to convince her to be in the show! Then she'd get over her stage fright once and for all. He'd be a good friend, and she'd be a better partner than ever!

They were getting their backpacks out of the trunk when Mike announced, "I think you should come up with a new act."

"I said I had stage fright," Nora said, a little huffy. "Remember?"

"Yeah, I remember," Mike said. "But that shouldn't stop you. You need to work through it!"

He had come up with some important points. "A talent show is one thing. What about when you need to do presentations in school? You can't afford to be scared then. You could ruin your report card!"

Nora turned toward her house. "Don't tease me," she said.

"I mean it!" Mike continued. "You can't be scared forever. What about when you grow up? When you run for president? You'll have to be on stages all the time!" If any kid he

Greenwood Public Library
310 S. Meridian St.
Greenwood, IN 46143

knew could be president, it was definitely Nora.

Mike's mom had started checking her phone as soon as she got out of the car. She didn't seem to be listening. Who knew she was going to save the day?

"You know, Nora, Mike's right," Mrs. Weiss chimed in. "Maybe you won't run for president. But public speaking will be part of whatever you decide to be when you grow up. You need to be comfortable in front of an audience. The only way to get past your fear is to practice."

Nora wasn't about to argue with Mike's mom.

And Mike kept hearing those words in his head: "Mike's right." Music to his ears!

"Magic can be scary, too," he reminded Nora. "But I don't let that stop me."

She sighed. "I couldn't be in the show, even if I wanted," Nora said. "I don't have a talent."

Mike's eyes bugged out. "You've got to be kidding me," he said. She was talented at *everything*.

"No, really. Think about it," Nora insisted. "Not the kind of talent I could do onstage. I'm good at school, right? But what could I do in a show? Take a math test?"

"You could play piano," Mike suggested. Even when she practiced, it sounded like a concert.

"How would I get a piano to school?" she asked.

There had to be a way, but whatever.

"Or you could walk on your hands," Mike said. "No one else at school can do that."

"Someone is already doing gymnastics," said Nora.

Mike rolled his eyes. Fine, he thought. If only someone would tell her what to do!

And then he knew who could. "Listen, I have a really good idea. Just trust me, okay? Can you come over for a while?"

Nora exhaled, like she was annoyed. She still agreed to come, though. "Let me tell my dad first," she said.

Mike found a bag of pretzels in the cabinet and poured himself some chocolate milk. Then he went upstairs to get his Magic 8 Ball. When Nora returned, he was sitting on the couch with it, asking questions.

"Will Nora change her mind?" Mike said.

He shook the Magic 8 ball and looked in the little window at the bottom. "You may rely on it," the ball said.

Nora flopped down next him. "Is that your good idea?" she asked, frowning. "It's not a crystal ball, Mike. It's a toy."

"It's from The White Rabbit, though," Mike reminded her. Which meant the toy might

carry a bit of magic. It might even help Nora
make a decision.

Mike handed her the ball and waited for
Nora to ask it a question. She turned it over in
her hands before she finally came up with
this: "Do I really have to be in the talent
show?"

She shook it up and checked the answer.
The Magic 8 Ball said, "It is decidedly so."

"Seriously?" Nora said.

"You can't be afraid forever," Mike pointed
out.

"I'm not doing the chicken dance again!"
Nora told the Magic 8 Ball.

"It can only answer yes or no questions,"
Mike reminded her.

Nora tried again. "Do I need to stick with
the chickens?"

"My sources say no," said the Magic 8 Ball.

"See?" said Mike. "It's giving good advice!"

Nora even smiled a little. "Okay," she said. She looked at the Magic 8 Ball intently. "But should I play the piano?"

Mike read the answer for her. "Outlook not so good."

"Should I walk on my hands?" she asked.

"Don't count on it," said the Magic 8 Ball.

Now, Mike spoke to the ball. He had some other acts in mind.

"Should Nora sing a song at the talent show?" he asked.

Nora objected. "I can't even carry a tune!"

The Magic 8 Ball totally agreed. "Very doubtful," it said.

Mike tried again. "Should she hula-hoop?"

"No!" said Nora, scowling. "That's as bad as the chicken dance!"

She grabbed the Magic 8 Ball. "My reply is no," it said.

"Whew!" said Nora.

Mike took the Magic 8 Ball back. "I have one more idea," he explained.

Mike didn't actually think Nora would want to sing or hula-hoop, but this next question was for real. He believed he'd get a real answer, too. The Magic 8 Ball had been telling them the truth. Maybe it had a bit of magic after all?

He knew one thing Nora could definitely do. Something she might even like doing, knowing Nora.

"Should Nora recite a poem at the talent show?" he asked.

Nora said, "That wouldn't be so bad. . . ."

I knew it! Mike thought.

But she wouldn't listen to him now. She'd only listen to the Magic 8 Ball.

The answer took a while to come to the surface, bobbing gently in the blue liquid.

"A poem?" Mike reminded the Magic 8 Ball.

The answer was clear. "As I see it, yes."

## Chapter 7
# SAVING LUCAS

**W**hen Mike walked into the gym the next day, other kids kept stopping him. "Your magic show was awesome," said one of the mimes, already in makeup.

"How did you do that thing with the ring?" asked a girl who used to be in Mike's class.

"It's a mystery," Mike replied, his smile stretching from ear to ear. He was getting all this attention now and the talent show hadn't even happened yet. What would happen next week, when people had seen the whole act, even the grand finale?

There was Adam, next to Nora, waving from a row of folding chairs. Mrs. Warren herded everyone else in that direction, saying, "Listen up, everyone! These seats are for the performers." The whole cast of the talent show was supposed to sit there, watching, until their turns came. Then parent volunteers would get kids where they needed to go.

Mike and Adam had a ton of stuff with them. The balloons and pins and tape. The pen and the bottle. A glass, a hat, and some coins for a trick they hadn't shown others yet. Mike had a surprise tucked into his magic hat. And they didn't even have their biggest prop yet, for the Disappearing Magician.

Maybe Nora can help us with that, Mike thought. She wasn't part of his act, but she was still a part of his team.

He couldn't ask her right now, though, because Nora was so nervous. She had her poem printed out on a piece of paper, and she kept reading it over and over. "'Twas brillig and the slithy toves did gyre and gimble in the wabe," she mumbled. She claimed it was in English, but Mike didn't know most of those words.

Mrs. Warren clicked the lights off and on to get everyone quiet. "I've put the acts in order," she told the group. "With ten before intermission and ten after." She started to read from her list. "We'll start with the mimes. Then the jugglers, and the chickens..." She went through the whole first half.

"You'll notice I've added some new acts to the second half of the show," Mrs. Warren went on. "Late entries. We'll see them for the

first time this afternoon. Then, to finish off the show, Mike Weiss and Adam Abbott. You don't mind going last, do you, boys?" she asked.

"Oh no, that's fine," Mike spoke up quickly.

Everyone knew that the last act was the most important! It was what the audience would remember most!

"Then we're ready to begin," said Mrs. Warren briskly.

The run-through took a while, since she was trying to get the sound and the lighting just right for each performance. Some kids were doing their homework while they waited to go on, but most kids were cheering on the other acts. When the lip-synchers came up, people were even singing along!

Then it was Nora's turn.

"Now for one of our new acts," said Mrs. Warren. "Nora Finn will be reciting a poem. Could you tell us the title, please?"

"Jabberwocky," said Nora. "By Lewis Carroll."

Nora took a deep breath as she walked to the microphone with her sheet of paper. Mike stood up and clapped like crazy. "You can do it, Nora!" he yelled.

Mike loved that no one would stop him from calling out for once. He also loved that, for the first time ever, Nora kind of needed him. As a magician would say, the tables were turned. With a friendly audience, Nora could get over her stage fright.

There was just one problem. Not everyone in the audience was friendly.

As soon as Mike's voice stopped echoing around the gym, another voice rang out. "A poem?" it jeered. "Come on! Who wants to hear that?"

Jackson Jacobs. What was *he* doing here?

Mike could see the paper shaking in Nora's hands. Luckily, she didn't really need it. She recited the whole poem by heart, never looking at Jackson. Mike still had no clue what the words meant, but he could tell that the poem was about a battle. Like whoever was fighting, Nora was brave.

Mike gave her a high-five as she walked back to her seat. "See?" he whispered. "Nothing to be scared of."

"Except Jackson," she replied quietly, looking in his direction.

"Thank you, Nora," said Mrs. Warren. "And we have one more late entry here. Jackson, are you ready?" she asked.

He tore onto the stage with a giant bag, like you'd use to carry hockey sticks. He zipped it open and took out a pair of big black boxing gloves, plus a punching bag.

Mrs. Warren's mouth looked like she had eaten something sour. "What can you tell us about your act?" she asked.

"Boxing," said Jackson, taking a couple of punches. "A demonstration." He whacked the bag with his glove. "This is my left hook, see?" he said. "And this is my punching bag." He turned it around so everyone could see that it

had a face, like a doll. "I call him Mike, since he's a dummy."

Mike turned the color of a tomato.

But Mrs. Warren had his back. "If you want to be in the talent show, Jackson, you'll need to come up with something more appropriate," she said firmly. "Nothing violent and nothing that insults another student. You should know better than that. Please return to your seat at once."

A storm cloud passed over Jackson's face, but he did as he was told. As he walked to his chair, he bashed Mike's chair with his bag.

Booing and bullying weren't allowed, Mike remembered. If he tried anything else, Jackson would be out of here.

Mrs. Warren kept a close eye on him as she called out the next name on her list. "Lucas?" she said.

"Yay, buddy!" Mike yelled as his first-grade friend took the stage. He was a one-man cheering squad today!

Lucas shook the hair out of his eyes, settled down on his stool, and got started. "Why was the math book unhappy?" he asked the crowd. He paused for a moment and answered his own question. "Because it had too many problems," he said. *Ba-dum-dum.*

"Oh, man," said Jackson. "That is so dumb."

Mike hoped Lucas couldn't hear him.

"Knock-knock," said Lucas.

"Who's there?" said Jackson loudly, in a baby voice.

*Everyone* heard him that time, Mike was sure.

Lucas shrank down on his stool a little. "Figs," he said.

"Figs who?" asked Jackson, still mocking.

When was Mrs. Warren going to stop him? Mike looked to her for help.

Oh, no! he thought. Why was she on her phone?

As the school secretary, he knew, Mrs. Warren had to handle all kinds of emergencies. But why here, and why now?

Lucas managed to finish his knock-knock joke. "Figs the doorbell, it's broken," he said, looking at the floor. He didn't knock on his stool this time, but he kept on going.

"Why did the chicken cross the road?" Lucas asked timidly.

Jackson waved his hand in the air. "I know! I know!" he said. "To get to the other side."

Lucas wasn't expecting audience participation. "No," he said, confused. "Um, it was because...um..." He'd lost his rhythm and suddenly, he looked really small up there, all by himself.

Mike remembered when he was small, like that. Even back then, Jackson was a problem.

Mike couldn't prove that Jackson had stolen his favorite fire engine, but the last time he'd seen it was at the last playdate they ever had together. And that snake in Mike's backyard? Who else would have put it there?

Mike wished for the kind of magic that would let him conjure up a red-hot lightning bolt. If he had one handy, he'd knock Jackson flat on the ground and keep him there till he sizzled!

But the other kind of magic—Mike's kind of magic—had stopped Jackson before. And it gave him more talents, actually, than he could ever perform in a show. When he was onstage, he felt strong and powerful, like a whole different Mike. Could he conjure up some of that courage in regular life?

Forget the cheering squad, Mike thought. I have to be the rescue squad for Lucas!

He'd never been a tattletale, but Jackson

was asking for this. He couldn't get away with heckling a little kid! Lucas was slinking off the stage when Mike marched up to Mrs. Warren. She was just putting her phone back in her pocket.

"Excuse me," Mike said politely. "But there's another emergency. Someone's been hurt. Can you help?"

## Chapter 8
# PRACTICE MAKES PERFECT

**W**ednesday's rehearsal was a little shorter, because everyone was getting used to the routine. A part of Mike wished he could stand onstage, under the lights, for longer. But he had some serious work to do at home. He had to make a prop for the Disappearing Magician!

After the practice, Adam and Nora both came back to his house. "Better keep your

coats on," Mike said as he led his friends into his garage. "It's freezing in here."

Usually, Mike's room was Magic Central, but today, they needed some space to stretch out. Mike led Adam and Nora past some boxes of holiday decorations and an exercise bike that no one used. There, in the back corner of the garage, was the box the Weisses' new fridge had come in.

"Here it is!" said Mike. The refrigerator box had to be eight feet tall, and all three kids could probably fit inside. When they cut off one of the sides, they would have a super-long, super-strong piece of cardboard.

He handed each of his friends a pair of scissors. Then he turned the box on its side, holding it in place while Adam and Nora started cutting from opposite ends.

"So Jackson's not doing an act?" Mike confirmed as they worked. "He wasn't at rehearsal."

Nora knew all the news. "He's not allowed to be in the show," she said. "Mrs. Warren kicked him out for bullying."

"Are you sure?" Mike asked suspiciously. Whenever he was supposed to face a consequence, Jackson wiggled out of it.

"Totally sure," said Nora. "He can't even come into the gym after school. She says she can't trust him."

Justice! Mike let out a breath he didn't even know he'd been holding. Telling on Jackson had been risky, but now the talent show would be Jackson-free! Nothing—and nobody—stood between Mike and a smash success!

Adam and Nora met up in the middle of the cardboard panel, and with one final snip, it fell to the basement floor. When they folded it in three parts, it would be able to stand up by itself.

Mike tried to picture it: He and Adam would carry this panel onstage, stand it up, and create an illusion so powerful that the audience wouldn't be able to believe their eyes!

He was so busy imagining this moment that he forgot what was happening right now.

"Mike?" said Nora. "What are we supposed to do now? We're waiting!"

Mike stopped spacing out. He couldn't believe *he* was supposed to give directions. He wasn't exactly used to being in charge!

"Now we get to paint it," Mike told Adam and Nora.

Everything they needed was out here. Paints from another art project. Some paintbrushes that were a little bent, but still usable. Mike even found some holey T-shirts they could use as smocks.

"On the count of three!" he said. "One ...
two ... three!" The three of them spattered paint
all over the cardboard panel till it was covered in
rainbow dots. The design had nothing to do with
the magic trick, but the cardboard panel looked
better now. Like it was in its own costume and
ready for the show.

There was only one problem. How were
they going to practice the Disappearing Magician? Mike and Adam couldn't rehearse it in

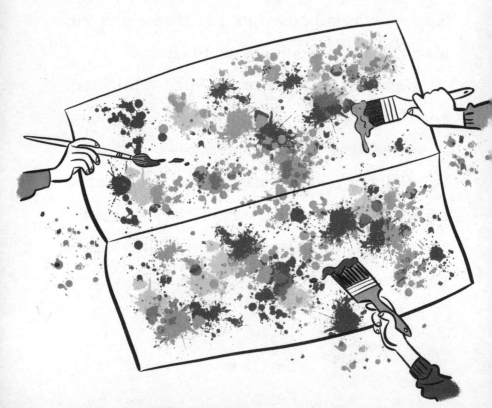

Mike's room, or even the basement. They needed a stage, and not the one at school. They couldn't take the chance that someone might see what they were up to.

"Could we get to school really early in the morning?" Adam asked, biting into a taco. Nora had left already, but Adam was staying for dinner.

"How early?" said Mike. "I mean, we'd have to get there before every single kid."

"True," Adam agreed. "What if we stay late after tomorrow's rehearsal?"

"I don't know," Mike said. "Can we be there by ourselves after dark?" Where else could they go? The auditorium at the junior high?

"Wait!" said Mike. "Maybe we could use the stage at The White Rabbit!"

Adam thought that could work. So, in the past few days, Mike had helped a friend. Stood up for a little kid. Led the way. Solved this problem! He was all about working magic in the talent show. But had some other strange magic been working on him, too? How was he suddenly so ... responsible?

♥   ♥   ♥

After a whole day of school, and after they had their last rehearsal and Mike's dad dropped Nora off at her piano lesson, Mike and Adam finally arrived at the magic shop. "I'll be back in an hour, okay, guys?" said Mr. Weiss.

Hopefully that would be enough time.

No one was at the front desk when they arrived, and there were no other customers in the store. The store felt totally different at the end of the day than on a Saturday morning. It was as if the whole shop, and all its secrets, belonged to Mike and Adam right now.

Mike felt funny about disturbing the quiet, but someone had to be here. "Mr. Zerlin?" he called out.

Suddenly, the magician was next to him. Had he appeared by magic? If anyone could do that, Mr. Zerlin could. Mike opened his mouth to ask about the stage, but then he noticed something. Mr. Zerlin's feet weren't touching the ground! He was carrying a quilt with both hands—it reached almost to his shoes—but between the quilt and the floor, Mike could see Mr. Zerlin's feet suspended in midair.

"How can I help you?" he asked Mike and Adam, floating slowly to the floor.

"How did you do that?" Adam asked.

Uh-oh, Mike thought. Mr. Zerlin didn't share his tricks with many people, and he barely knew Adam. But Mr. Zerlin was kind to Mike's friend. "Someday I'll show you," he said, without saying when.

"So, I was wondering," Mike said, "if we could use your stage to practice the Disappearing Magician."

One minute Mr. Zerlin was all mysterious, and the next minute he was encouraging the boys like a coach. "Of course!" he said, leading the way downstairs and flicking on the lights. "Tell me, when is the show?"

"Tomorrow!" Mike said. He wouldn't get much sleep tonight. He dropped his bag of props on the floor, and Adam leaned the cardboard panel against the wall.

"And you're only practicing now?" asked Mr. Zerlin gravely.

Adam handled that one. "Oh, no! We practiced, like, every minute last weekend. And every day after school. We've gone through the Disappearing Magician over and over again. But we really need to do it on a real stage, right? We need a final run-through."

Mr. Zerlin's face crinkled into a smile. "You can never be too prepared," he said.

We know! Mike thought impatiently. "Can we show you part of our act?" he said.

Mr. Zerlin nodded and crossed his arms, like a signal that he was ready.

Just like he would in the show, Adam brought a table to the center of the stage and placed a glass on it. Then he put a baseball cap upside down on the rim of the glass, and slipped a nickel between the cap and the rim, where no one in the audience could see it. The coin was slanted into the glass, and the hat was holding it in place.

Mike stepped forward, took a deep breath, and used his best performer's voice. "See these coins?" he asked the empty room, showing a handful of quarters he took out of his pockets. "Just regular old quarters, right?" He paused for the part where the audience would agree. Then he stuck his finger in the air like he was saying, "Hold on one second!"

"Watch carefully as I drop these coins into the hat," he told the invisible audience. "One of them will fall through the hat and into the glass."

He dropped the quarters into the hat, one by one, making sure that the original coin stayed stuck. Then, when the audience couldn't stand the suspense, he dropped a quarter and moved the hat at exactly the same time. It had taken Mike a while to get this timing perfect, but he did it flawlessly. It looked like the quarter he dropped was the same quarter that hurtled into the glass! Really, though, the one that fell was the one that had been waiting to all along.

Mike imagined the applause and took a tiny bow. "Thank you, thank you," he said modestly.

# COIN DROP

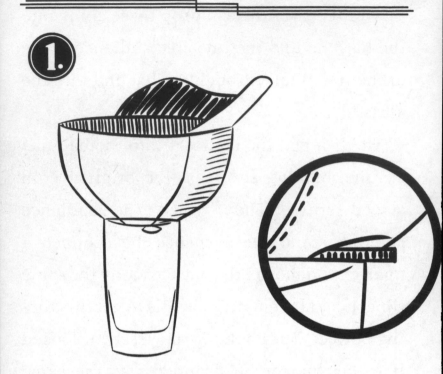

*B*EGIN BY SETTING A GLASS ON A TABLE, WITH A BASEBALL CAP (OR SOME OTHER HAT) UPSIDE DOWN ON THE RIM. THEN, BALANCE A COIN ON THE RIM, UNDER THE HAT, WHERE NOBODY CAN SEE IT. THE HAT WILL HOLD THE COIN IN PLACE AT AN ANGLE.

TO PERFORM THIS TRICK, YOU'LL NEED SEVERAL COINS OF THE SAME VALUE—QUARTERS WORK BEST.

**2.** TELL YOUR AUDIENCE THAT YOU WILL DROP THE COINS INTO THE HAT. ONE OF THEM, YOU SAY, WILL GO THROUGH THE HAT! START DROPPING THE COINS, ONE BY ONE, TO BUILD SUSPENSE.

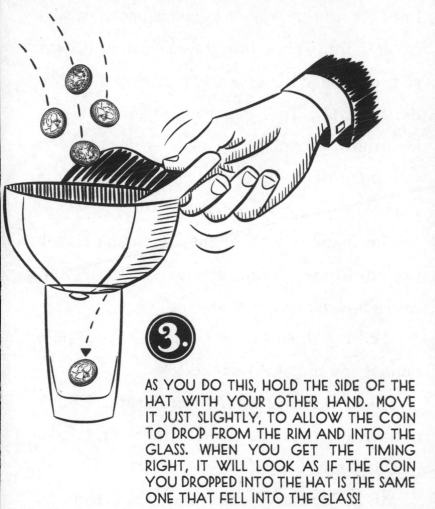

**3.** AS YOU DO THIS, HOLD THE SIDE OF THE HAT WITH YOUR OTHER HAND. MOVE IT JUST SLIGHTLY, TO ALLOW THE COIN TO DROP FROM THE RIM AND INTO THE GLASS. WHEN YOU GET THE TIMING RIGHT, IT WILL LOOK AS IF THE COIN YOU DROPPED INTO THE HAT IS THE SAME ONE THAT FELL INTO THE GLASS!

Mr. Zerlin nodded. "Nicely done," he said, stroking his chin.

Mike could feel himself blushing again, but this time it wasn't because Jackson was trash-talking. This time, it was because he was so proud! He'd never really performed for Mr. Zerlin before. This was even bigger than performing at school!

"Looks like you're ready to take it on the road," the magician added.

The road? Mike thought. He wasn't traveling anywhere, except school. Only Mr. Zerlin's act went on the road.

"Tell me this," said Mr. Zerlin. "What happens if you make a mistake?"

There was only one answer to that. "I won't make any mistakes," Mike said. "I practiced, just like you said!"

Mr. Zerlin's bright gaze met his. "Think on your feet. Stay calm. You must be prepared for anything. Every audience tests you in a different way."

Mike swallowed. Did Mr. Zerlin think he couldn't do it?

"I *know* you can do it," the magician said, like he knew what Mike was thinking. "But remember: Expect the unexpected, and make it into magic."

Mike nodded, taking it all in.

"And the finale?" Mr. Zerlin said. "Can I see?"

By now, Adam was good at following cues. He brought out the cardboard panel, and the two boys took their positions onstage.

## ·.⁺ₒ* **Chapter 9** .ₓ✳.ₒ*
# THE BIG NIGHT

**I**t was almost showtime!

The talent show cast was lined up in a classroom, ready to file into the gym and take their
seats. Mrs. Warren was giving an inspirational
speech, while a few kids sneaked in some last-
minute practice. Mike couldn't get the lip-
synchers' music out of his head!

Mike was wearing sneakers, but his stomach was doing flip-flops.

He wasn't nervous, he told himself. It was just that he hadn't had dinner. Mrs. Warren ordered pizza for the whole group, but who could eat? Mike was only hungry for his turn onstage!

Adam was right next to him. Mike whispered, "I'll be back in a minute, okay?" When no one was watching, he darted into the hallway. He had to know what was happening in the gym!

He slipped past the ticket line and poked his head in through the open door. He was shocked when he saw the crowd. Almost every seat was full! Mike gulped. This was way bigger than he'd expected.

As he rushed back to the classroom, the reflection in a window caught his eye. There was Ms. Scott, welcoming a group of parents. There were some people taking off their coats. And there was a magician.

Wait a minute! Mike thought. Was someone copying his act?

It took Mike a second to realize he was looking at himself. With his dark shirt and his magic hat, he looked like the real deal. His stomach did another somersault. He knew how the whole school would see him after tonight.

Mike hadn't missed much. Mrs. Warren was still going on and on. "Not only will we put on a wonderful show," she said, "but we will begin a wonderful tradition for our school. . . ."

The gymnast was standing in front of Adam with a mouthful of gum, blowing bubbles like she wasn't worried at all. "Want to pop a bubble?" she asked the boys. "For good luck?"

Who could say no to good luck? Adam and Mike took turns popping until Mrs. Warren said, "Ready to go!" Mike wished he could wipe off his sticky fingers, but he was out of time.

As the cast members settled into their special seats, Mike scanned the gym for his parents. His mom was working late, his dad had a meeting, then someone had to pick up his grandma. Were they even here? he wondered. What if they missed it? His grandma had to see him in Houdini's hat! Mike was still searching for them when the lights went down.

The talent show started out quiet, with the mimes. But by the time the funky chickens came onstage, the crowd was clapping and stomping its feet! Mrs. Warren gave the kids a thumbs-up just before intermission. "Keep up the good work," she told them. "It's going like clockwork!"

The sound of applause made Mike hungry again. Pretty soon now, the clapping would be for him! And who was that, waving from the back row? His grandma! She blew him a kiss, and Mike tipped his hat. Tonight, he would make his family proud!

The performers were getting restless by the time the second act got started. The juggler, who had already gone on, passed around a beanbag like a hot potato. Someone else started a game of telephone. Mrs. Warren glared and said, "Shhhh!"

Adam didn't get involved. "You okay?" Mike whispered.

Adam nodded. "I can't wait to get up there!" he said. Mike knew exactly how he felt.

Just when it seemed like it would never be their turn, a parent volunteer helped Mike and Adam carry their stuff to a waiting area backstage. From there, they watched Nora charm the audience. When she recited her poem, Mike knew all the parents were wishing their kids could do that. Nora's voice was creaky, but she was smiling, too. Her friends, the chickens, bawk-bawked for her when she was done.

Then Mrs. Warren's announcement rang out. "And for the last act of the night, from the fourth grade: Mike Weiss, Man of Magic, and his absolutely astonishing assistant, Adam Abbott."

Mike stepped out of the shadows and into the light.

His music came on, proclaiming his arrival.

And seriously, for one second, Mike thought he was going to throw up.

The lights were really bright tonight. So bright that he couldn't even see the faces in the audience.

And was the music so loud in the rehearsals? Mike couldn't remember.

Flustered, he lost his footing. He tripped and fell, right there in front of everyone.

The disappearing magician? Yes, he would love to disappear! His parents had to be here somewhere. Their car was parked outside. They could take him home right now....

But should they?

The whole gym was quiet, except for Mike's blaring music. In that blur of light, there was a whole gym full of people waiting to see his act. It was everything Mike had ever wanted. Yeah, he'd really *wanted* this! He wasn't going to miss his chance.

Mike picked himself up off the floor. He strode over to Adam, took a balloon from his hands, and blew it up. "Just a regular old balloon," he told the audience. "Like you'd have at your birthday party." The familiar words calmed him down a little. As he spoke, he slipped the tape on, where no one could see it.

Adam handed him the pin, and Mike said, "Let's see if I can pop the balloon with this pin, okay?" With an extra-big gesture, Mike stuffed the pin into the balloon . . . and it popped. What happened? Suddenly, Mike knew. He'd missed the tape. Was it because his hands were shaking? Was it because the lights were blinding him? Was he having stage fright himself? What would he tell Nora to do?

Mike took a deep breath. "I think I'll try something else," he said with a big fake grin. "How does that sound?" He couldn't lose the audience yet! He still had a bunch of great tricks lined up!

Luckily, he had a great partner, too. Adam didn't freak out. He just jumped off the stage and walked down one of the aisles, asking, "Could we borrow a ring from someone, please?" Smoothly, he moved Mike toward the next trick.

Mike's vision was adjusting to the light now. He could see Adam moving to the back of the gym. He could see when a lady gave Adam a ring off her finger. He could see the stripes on her hat. He could see who was sitting next to her, too.

Jackson.

Kicked out of the show, but not kicked out of the audience, Mike realized too late.

What had Mr. Zerlin said? Every audience tested you in its own way?

Adam delivered the ring, and Mike dropped his voice, like he was sharing a secret with the audience. "Watch this ring defy the laws of gravity!" he dared them. He took the pen from his pocket, dropped the ring on it, and stared at it with lowered eyebrows. If his fierce look could have worked magic, it would have.

As Mike moved the pen away from his body, the thread snagged on his sticky fingers . . . and ripped. And since the trick depended on a hidden thread, the ring clattered onto the stage floor.

What kind of magic act was this? the audience had to be wondering. Just one mistake after another. Was it supposed to be funny? Mike could hear some confused laughter.

Then a voice said what tons of people were probably thinking. "This act stinks!"

Jackson, of course.

Mike could feel his shirt getting damp with sweat. He'd had a second chance, and a third, but things just kept getting worse! If he couldn't do a decent magic act at the talent show, what *could* he do?

He stood up a little straighter. He still had this. He'd show everyone!

The next trick was supposed to be the Floating Pen. But that one relied on a thread, too, and suddenly that scared Mike. Better to skip it, he thought.

He picked up the baseball cap, and that's all Adam needed to see. Instead of the Floating Pen, he set up the Coin Drop in a flash. He put the glass on a table and the hat in the glass, hiding the coin on the edge.

Adam did everything perfectly. Mike couldn't blame him for what happened next. But somehow, when he began to do the trick, Mike knocked the glass over. Now people were totally cracking up, like he was some kind of comedian.

Mike tuned them out. He really did. He would finish this trick if it killed him!

He was setting it up again, still holding himself together, when a "Boo!" roared out from the back of the gym. Jackson again.

He had his own trick up his sleeve, and it wasn't magic. It was just plain mean.

Jackson stood up on his seat, waving a deck of cards in the air.

"Hey, Magic Man!" he yelled out so everyone could hear. "Since you have such special . . . *powers* . . . I know you can tell me this." He took a card from the deck and stuffed it in his pocket.

"What card did I pick out?" he jeered. "Huh?"

If this was a test, Mike thought, he now knew his grade.

This was an epic fail.

## Chapter 10
# SHOWTIME

**M**ike couldn't see things that were invisible, or detect what you were thinking, or predict the future. He wasn't, like, some kind of wizard, he thought bitterly. He couldn't make magical things happen in the world. He could only make it *seem* that way.

What Jackson was asking then? Impossible.

Mike stood there, sweating under the lights. If this was during the school day, or rehearsal, a teacher would have rescued him. But who was in charge of Jackson now?

And even if someone came and hauled Jackson away, his question still hung in the air. What was the card? Mike had no idea.

But people wanted to know the answer. Every eye in the gym was on him.

Expect the unexpected, Mr. Zerlin had said. Well, this was definitely unexpected. Too bad Mr. Zerlin hadn't told him what to do next. Make it into magic? How was that supposed to work? Mike would have to figure it out while the whole gym watched.

How did you make something into magic, anyway? You took something ordinary, like popping a balloon, and changed it. Tweaked the situation so that something happened that *couldn't* happen or *shouldn't* happen.

What was the one thing that couldn't happen here? That Mike would pick the right card. There was just no way.

But what would a magician do? A magician would turn everything upside down.

Would he take a wild guess?

Hey, it wasn't like Mike had a lot of other choices. So he closed his eyes, like he was thinking. He pulled his hat—Houdini's hat—down over his face. And then, out of nowhere, he knew it. He didn't know how, but he could see the card in his mind.

He stepped to the edge of the stage and spoke to Jackson. "Ten of hearts," said Mike. "That's what's in your pocket."

Jackson took the card out gleefully, like he'd been waiting for this moment all week.

But his gloating smile changed when he looked at it. "You've got to be kidding me," he said, slamming it into his leg.

"It's the ten of hearts!" the lady next to him confirmed.

Jackson tore the card into pieces and slumped in his chair.

Mike had tricked Jackson before, but this time was different.

This time it wasn't a trick.

The audience clapped and whistled. The talent show kids stood up and cheered!

Jackson was down, and suddenly, Mike was on fire. His act wasn't over yet!

Instinctively, he knew what to do next. He took the hat off his head and peered in. He turned it upside down and shook it out. "Nothing there, right?" he asked the audience. People shook their heads, agreeing it was empty.

Mike put it back on his head and walked across the stage. Then his expression changed, and everyone could read it: Something was inside the hat now. He could feel it!

Mike removed the hat again, and took out some tiny squares of colored paper, like confetti. He showed them to the audience, in the palm of his hand. That's cool, their faces told him.

That was only the beginning.

Mike grabbed the confetti and shook his hand in the air. Suddenly, he was holding an armful of streamers!

Their eyes opened wider, and that's when Mike knew. He was back on track. They were with him. *This* was his moment. He'd just arrived a different way.

He'd skipped the Floating Pen before, but he bet he could carry it off now. He walked over to Adam and asked for the plastic bottle. Then he took the other pen from his shirt pocket and told the audience what to expect. "I will drop this pen into the bottle," he told them dramatically. "And then I will control it with my mind."

It was a big promise, he knew. After what just happened, though, anything was possible.

Holding the bottle close to his chest, he dropped the pen through the top. Then he moved the bottle slowly away from his body, watching the pen the whole time. Sure enough, it floated in midair, hovering eerily until it reached the top. The audience went wild!

Crazy how things could change so fast, thought Mike. One minute, everything was all wrong, and the next minute everything was completely right. So, what made the difference?

Maybe there was still some magic clinging to the hat he'd inherited from Houdini.

Maybe it was just one lucky guess.

Or maybe it was something he'd done for himself.

He couldn't explain how he knew what the card was, but he could explain what happened before that. He'd worked hard. He'd stayed cool, acted confident, and kept an open mind. And after all of that . . . he made another kind of magic.

Suddenly, like that, he knew his magic word. It had been right there in front of him all along.

There was one trick left in their program now: the grand finale. Mike dragged the cardboard panel to the edge of the stage, almost in the wings. Then he put his hand on the edge of the panel and spoke again to the audience.

"When the music comes on," Mike said, "I will drag this cardboard panel to the center of the stage. And then, if everything goes right— which I really hope it will, this time—you *will* be surprised."

The audience laughed in the right place, and looked excited in the right place, too. It was sort of good that he'd messed up so badly,

Mike thought. Now everyone was on the edge of their seats.

The music didn't seem quite as loud now. When it started, Mike ducked behind the panel, then popped his head out of the side so the audience could catch a final glimpse of him.

It was a song with a slow beat, and the panel moved slowly across the stage with the rhythm. When the music finally stopped, the panel was in the center of the stage, its painted dots glowing under the bright lights. The audience could see his hands steadying the cardboard, making sure it would stand up straight.

Backstage, though, Mike was running as fast as he could. He was probably breaking some school records, he thought—not to mention some rules—but no one was timing him. No one even knew he was here! People thought he was still behind that panel.

He tore around the storage area and through a door at the rear of the stage. Then he raced into the hallway, through the empty school, and toward the back door of the gym.

The music stopped, and the hands behind the panel disappeared. There was a second of silence, then the audience heard an unexpected voice from the last row of seats behind them.

It was Mike, in the triumphant moment he'd been dreaming of all week. Actually, it was even sweeter than what he'd dreamed of, since he'd really struggled to get here.

Hundreds of heads whipped around to see him standing there. To hear him call out his magic word for the first time ever.

It was sort of about magic, but more about what magic had taught him.

On a cold, dark night, his voice was like a rocket in the school gym: "Believe!"

# The End

# The DISAPPEARING MAGICIAN

**D**O YOU HAVE A HELPER YOU CAN TRUST? THEN YOU CAN PERFORM THE DISAPPEARING MAGICIAN (WITH SOME PRACTICE)! YOU'LL ALSO NEED A LARGE PIECE OF CARDBOARD, BIG ENOUGH TO HIDE TWO KIDS AND STRONG ENOUGH TO STAND ON ITS OWN, WITH A TINY PEEPHOLE CUT INTO IT.

**1.** PLACE THE CARDBOARD ON THE FAR SIDE OF A STAGE, SO THAT PART OF IT IS VISIBLE TO THE AUDIENCE AND PART OF IT IS HIDDEN BACKSTAGE. YOUR HELPER SHOULD STAND BEHIND THE CARDBOARD, OUT OF SIGHT OF THE AUDIENCE.

**2.** BEGIN BY WALKING TOWARD THE CARDBOARD, THEN STEPPING BEHIND IT YOURSELF. YOUR HELPER WILL PUT ONE OF HIS HANDS ON TOP OF THE CARDBOARD, AND THE OTHER ON THE SIDE THAT THE AUDIENCE CAN SEE. THE AUDIENCE WILL THINK THESE ARE YOUR HANDS, BECAUSE THEY DON'T KNOW THE HELPER IS THERE.

POP YOUR HEAD OUT FROM BEHIND THE CARDBOARD, SO THE AUDIENCE CAN SEE YOU. THEN CROUCH BACK DOWN, SO THEY CAN'T SEE YOU, AND STEP PAST YOUR HELPER INTO THE STAGE WINGS.

YOUR HELPER WILL REMAIN HIDDEN, WITH ONLY HIS HANDS SHOWING, AND DRAG THE CARDBOARD TO THE CENTER OF THE STAGE. HE WILL TAKE HIS TIME SETTING UP THE CARDBOARD, MAKING SURE IT WILL STAND UP WITHOUT FALLING.

**4.** THE AUDIENCE WILL EXPECT TO SEE YOU BEHIND THAT CARDBOARD. BUT YOU'RE NOT THERE! YOU ARE QUICKLY SLIPPING OUT THE SIDE OR A BACKSTAGE EXIT DOOR. THEN YOU'RE RUNNING AROUND THE THEATER FROM THE OUTSIDE (OR THROUGH AN INSIDE HALLWAY IF POSSIBLE). VERY QUIETLY, YOU'LL ENTER THE THEATER THROUGH THE BACK DOOR AND STAND IN THE AISLE.

YOUR HELPER IS THE ONLY ONE WHO WILL SEE—THROUGH THE PEEPHOLE—WHEN YOU ARRIVE AT THE THEATER'S BACK DOOR. EVERY OTHER EYE IN THE AUDIENCE WILL BE ON THE STAGE.

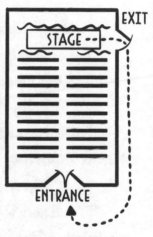

EXIT

STAGE

ENTRANCE

EXIT

**5.** WHEN YOUR HELPER SEES YOU, HE WILL REMOVE HIS HANDS FROM THE CARDBOARD. THEN IT IS YOUR JOB TO GET THE FULL ATTENTION OF THE AUDIENCE BY GIVING THEM A GREAT SURPRISE—YELLING OUT YOUR MAGIC WORD FROM THE BACK OF THE ROOM! WHEN THE AUDIENCE TURNS AROUND, THE HELPER CAN QUICKLY LEAVE THE STAGE, SCOOTING UNDER THE BACKDROP BEHIND HIM.

JUN 2 4 2015

Thank you for reading this
FEIWEL AND FRIENDS book.
The Friends who made

possible are:

**Jean Feiwel**, *Publisher*

**Liz Szabla**, *Editor in Chief*

**Rich Deas**, *Senior Creative Director*

**Holly West**, *Associate Editor*

**Dave Barrett**, *Executive Managing Editor*

**Nicole Liebowitz Moulaison**, *Production Manager*

**Lauren A. Burniac**, *Editor*

**Anna Roberto**, *Associate Editor*

**Christine Barcellona**, *Administrative Assistant*

FOLLOW US ON FACEBOOK OR VISIT US ONLINE AT
MACKIDS.COM.

*Our books are friends for life.*